THE INCREDIBLE DIARY OF...

Fantastic Adventures

Edited By Jenni Harrison

Young Writers

First published in Great Britain in 2023 by:

Young Writers
Remus House
Coltsfoot Drive
Peterborough
PE2 9BF
Telephone: 01733 890066
Website: www.youngwriters.co.uk

Printed and bound in the UK by BookPrintingUK
Website: www.bookprintinguk.com
YB0549F

FOREWORD

Dear Diary,

You will never guess what I did today! Shall I tell you? Some primary school pupils wrote some diary entries and I got to read them, and they were EXCELLENT!

Here at Young Writers we created some bright and funky worksheets along with fun and fabulous (and free) resources to help spark ideas and get inspiration flowing. And it clearly worked because WOW!! I can't believe the adventures I've been reading about. Real people, make believe people, dogs and unicorns, even objects like pencils all feature and these diaries all have one thing in common – they are JAM-PACKED with imagination, all squeezed into 100 words!

Here at Young Writers we want to pass our love of the written word onto the next generation and what better way to do that than to celebrate their writing by publishing it in a book! It sets their work free from homework books and notepads and puts it where it deserves to be – **OUT IN THE WORLD!**

Each awesome author in this book should be super proud of themselves, and now they've got proof of their imagination, their ideas and their creativity in black and white, to look back on in years to come!

CONTENTS

Evelyn Butler (11)	60
Ania O'Neill (9)	61
Florence Cawdron (9)	62
Nell Pringle Rogers (8)	63
Stella Packer (7)	64
Francesca Brooke (11)	65
Louisa Yelland (10)	66
Monty Wheeler (9)	67
Imogen Hardy (9)	68
Marnie Clark (8)	69
Declan Provino (9)	70
Hadley Provino (11)	71
Peter Gray (10)	72
Ida Cobanoglu (8)	73
Charles Dupont (8)	74
Bluebell Gorden-Malone (10)	75
Nia Tainton (8)	76
Ernie Carter Croucher (8)	77
Alexander Bamber (9)	78
Selma Yoruk (7)	79
Afsana Ahmed (9)	80
Liam O'Healai (10)	81
Alex Ardalan (9)	82
Idris Weston (8)	83
Suki Slater (9)	84
Sophie Dempster (8)	85
Georgia Freud (8)	86
Elodie Sack (9)	87
Penny Mountford (10)	88
Benjamin Chubb (8)	89
Lara Ostroumoff (8)	90
Julia Mammadova (10)	91
Bianca Vecchi (9)	92
Arvin Kaygisiz (8)	93
Charis Lalobo (9)	94
Tuna Chakat (9)	95
Aya Sophie Lim (10)	96
George Woolston (7)	97
Sophie Tolmunen (9)	98
Josephine Vannier (9)	99
Liza Dyshlyuk (8)	100
Elisabeth Petova (8)	101
Antia Corrales (9)	102

Emilia Ostroumoff (8)	103
Ottilie Taylor Goldsmith (7)	104
Latifa Mursal (9)	105
Maggie Lumsdon (8)	106
Poppy Probert (9)	107
Sara Garcia Ciolczyk (9)	108
Diana Springs (8)	109
Micah Croll-Mensah (9)	110
Tate Patterson-Waugh (9)	111
Hashim Ahmed (9)	112
Sebastian Radosz (9)	113
Maddie Pretto (9)	114
Erick Fereira Sagredo (8)	115

Riverside Community Primary School, St Budeaux

Maximilian Dettlaff (9)	116
Liliana Strzelczak (10)	117
Jacob Guichard (9)	118
Logan Monk (10)	119
Melissa Rowe (10)	120

Sacred Heart RC Primary School, Blackburn

Aliyah Kamal (10)	121
Usman Asad (10)	122
Shanelle Ofosu (10)	123
Abeeha Naheed (9)	124
Amaya (9)	125
Huria Naveed (9)	126
Hamna Arooj (9)	127

Spring Cottage Primary School, Hull

Mia Clark (8)	128
Aoife Dodd (7)	129
Ellie Todd (8)	130
Matilda Rennard (8)	131
Aiza Mannan (8)	132
Liyaa Hawar (8)	133
Isabella Coutts (7)	134

Swimbridge Primary School, Swimbridge

Ella Picken (9)	135
Charile Parry (11)	136
Alfie-Joe Blackmore (6)	137
Penny Orr (7)	138
Amelia Darch (9)	139
Tom V H (10)	140
Anise Grant (7)	141
Leila Pavord (11)	142
Alex Ward (5)	143

THE STORIES

Hmmm What Was That?

Dear Diary,

Yesterday an extremely interesting (tiny bit funny as well) event happened. I was walking with my friend when a very cute cat jumped out. Immediately I started to yowl and screech. Then it disappeared. It reappeared 10ft away from where it had originally started. At first I screamed in shock and then Ashley screamed. Despite the situation, I burst out laughing.

"That was just a hologram, right?" said Ashely.

"I dunno, probably," I replied.

When we walked past that spooky mysterious place, we ran as fast as we could. We've never solved the mystery!

Amelia Din (11)

Green Crescent Primary School, Basford

Educational Medical Centre

Dear Diary,

Today I gathered enough money to make a medical centre for children in need, the children who have suffered from different diseases and need treatment every single day. That is why they can't go to school. That is why I have been working on gathering enough money to build this medical centre for the last three years. This medical centre will have an educational school, which provides special hard-working teachers who give them a special environment in which they learn different skills and fight against their diseases. I hope that this project is a success.

Aadil Umair Rahim (9)

Green Crescent Primary School, Basford

Luck Dragon

Dear Diary,

My name is Gemma, or as people call me, Gemma Dilemma. You see, I have a cloud above my head raining bad luck on me every second so today was the best thing that happened to me! I lingered my way to school very slowly then something caught my eye.

"What's this?" I asked myself, picking it up.

It was a white jar with red writing.

"Luck Dragon," I read.

Poof!

A small red dragon appeared. Realising it was late, I carefully placed the dragon in my pocket and sprinted off. It gave me luck all day!

Inara Mahmud (8)

Green Crescent Primary School, Basford

Hadeeqah's Favourite Eid

Dear Diary,
"Eid Mubarak!" my dad yelled.
We all got ready and went to the hall that my uncle had booked and spent time with my family. We played musical chairs for the elderly, middle-aged and kids. My grandma and two cousins won. When we played pass the parcel I thought I was going to get the prize, but just got a small toy instead. We went to my grandad's house, it was night. We ate food and everyone went home.
I got £110 Eid money and two amazing presents from my cousin Samiah!
Could this day get any better?

Hadeeqah Sohail (9)
Green Crescent Primary School, Basford

The Amazing Adventure

Dear Diary,

In Dovedale Park, me and Harry Potter met! Then something bad happened...

There was a very big earthquake! That was not good... Then a question hit us. How on earth were we going to save the Earth? Then we thought of a solution, to use our magic wands to save the world! So, we used our wands...

"Hocus pocus. Abracadabra." And more spells to be muttered. Slowly, we saved the world with a few flicks of our wands! That was it. We did it. Harry Potter and I set off for our next adventure lurking in the shadows.

Harime Badar (10)

Green Crescent Primary School, Basford

Duncan Goes Diving

Dear Diary,

Today I visited my garden to pick some fresh apples and suddenly I got sucked up by a mysterious black hole. Two days later, I reached Switzerland! Over there, there were many tropical oceans, seas, streams and rivers. I was in great astonishment. After that, I found my way to a haunted house. It was dark but not scary. I visited the sea again and I went diving. It was deep but I could swim in it. I took a deep breath and jumped into the fabulous, tropical water. I opened my eyes to discover other beautiful fish.

Waail Saoudi (8)

Green Crescent Primary School, Basford

The Adventure Of Mubaarak

One day, in a city, everyone was fine until a bad guy came to wreck the town. Someone could save it and it was me, Mubaarak, the brave warrior. I had a golden sword and a silver shield and I had sparkling armour. Then I said to the monster, "Stop, please, you're wrecking the town."
But it didn't want to listen so there was one choice, to fight. The fierce monster threw me on the floor. I didn't give up and kept fighting. Soon, I won and the monster had to stop wrecking the town. So he won't be back.

Mubaarak Raji (7)
Green Crescent Primary School, Basford

Mr Snowman

Dear Diary,

I went to the desert and saw Mr Snowman. Mr Snowman never melts. He is happy because he never melts. Mr Snowman is a Muslim. Then Mr Snowman went to London. In London, he saw the Eye of London and Big Ben. He went to Buckingham Palace. After, he went to Drayton Manor. After Drayton Manor, he went to Go Ape. Now Mr Snowman is going home, to the desert. He went home on an aeroplane. Sadly, I had to say goodbye and go back to England. I'm just going to say goodbye Mr Snowman and everyone.

Salahuddeen Mahboob Alam (8)

Green Crescent Primary School, Basford

Tariq And The Wild Beast

Dear Diary,

One day I woke to the roar of an unknown beast. I got dressed and looked out of the window but there was nothing there. I tiptoed out of my house and suddenly a huge shadow fell over me. I looked up and saw a gigantic beast. Then, for three days, I searched him for his weakness while he was sleeping. I found out that his weakness was that he always went into a deep sleep for one hour. I seized the next opportunity and, taking my sword, I attacked him from behind, striking him in the neck.

Muhammad Mustafa Sheikh (9)

Green Crescent Primary School, Basford

Simon's Disappearance

On a spooky and dark night, I was being chased by a group of skeletons because I betrayed the group. Then I fell into a deep dark ditch where an ancient mummy was peacefully sleeping. Frightened, I tiptoed around the mummy, trying to look for a way out of the cave. Then all of a sudden, the mummy woke up and ran at me and all that was left were my bones...

Years on, unsuspecting archaeologists discovered the remains of me and he built me back but he regretted it because I soon invaded the whole city.

Ahmed Humayun (9)
Green Crescent Primary School, Basford

Terragon And The Dragon

Dear Diary,

Yesterday I saw a ferocious fire-breathing dragon. He had three heads, six legs and four eyes. When I saw him, it was next to a grey, dark cave. I was on a trip so did not know what was going on. I was walking to the hotel when a crooked, old man told me about the dragon. So I invited him in. He said, "The dragon can burn a whole hotel at one time. He likes to stamp on houses at night and terrorise people."

Today, I will go on an adventure. Can I, Terragon, succeed?

Muhammad Hashir (8)

Green Crescent Primary School, Basford

The Hero Saves The Day!

Dear Diary,
Today I saw something so amazing, it was a hero and there were baddies. So the baddies were trying to steal from a shop. When I called the hero, he came in two minutes! I told him what they were doing and where they were doing it. When he came, the shopkeeper was tied up to a chair in the shop. The hero saved him and fought the baddies. They got so scared that they went running away and never came back. The mayor found out about this and gave the hero a big, shiny, gold medal.

Mariya Faisal (10)
Green Crescent Primary School, Basford

Danny And The Crazy Mutant Monkeys

One day, I was at school doing science. Just that second, about 70 green-eyed monkeys were staring at me like they were crazy. During break time, I went to check it out and I got one banana and gave it to the monkeys. The monkeys turned it into a mutant banana. I knew that something was wrong so I kicked the monkeys on a nearby road but somehow they teleported back. I was amazed to see what had happened. I brought them home and raised them. After 7 years, we went on a holiday and were happy.

Gibril Kaira (8)
Green Crescent Primary School, Basford

Jack And The Beast

Dear Diary,

Once upon a time, there was a beast that would stink and make people not breathe but then I decided to defeat the beast. So I went to where the beast lived which was in a dump and with one strike, *boom*, the beast was destroyed. So then I went back to the town to tell them that they were free and then people called my name in joy because I destroyed the horribly stinky beast. Now I was one of the best people in the world because of the big job I did and I was great.

Ameena Ahmeti (7)
Green Crescent Primary School, Basford

A Day In The Life Of Super Talhah

I am only 10 years old but there is something special about me. It is that I am a superhero. But it's a secret. Nobody knows and nobody should ever know. Otherwise, I will become very shy from other people knowing I am a superhero and everyone will ask me lots of questions. I am a very shy boy and do not like too many questions. Otherwise, I would go crazy, as crazy as a lab scientist. Actually, crazier than a lab scientist, crazier than anything. It would be very hard to calm me down.

Khadija Zia (8)
Green Crescent Primary School, Basford

Trapped

Dear Diary,

Yesterday was the scariest day of my life. I was stuck in the room. I couldn't open my eyes. Something was shining so bright that if I didn't cover my eyes, I would go blind. I didn't know how long I'd been there. There was no difference between day and night. I snoozed off after a bit. It was the first dream I'd ever had. There was a kitten in front of me. It was pushing a key towards me. I picked it up and pushed it into a door. I was finally free.

Ayesha Saeed (11)
Green Crescent Primary School, Basford

Lost In Space

Dear Diary,

I passed my space test and went on the Resolute, a satellite spaceship. In the Resolute, alien robots started attacking us in space. We had to split up and leave the Resolute. Soon all of us landed on the same unknown planet. It was snow and ice everywhere and it was cold. Then Judy, my sister, fell in the ice and then the ice froze. With my mum and sister injured, my dad tried to break the ice but failed. Then he found out that I was on a different part of the planet.

Zain Khan (9)
Green Crescent Primary School, Basford

YoungWriters
— Est 1991 —

My Trip To Star City

Dear Diary,

My name is Asma and my surname is Marjan. One day, I went on a trip with my dad, brother, little sister and me. We went to a very fun place called Star City. It has lots of places in it like arcades and stuff like that. We went to something called Gravity and Star City was in Birmingham. My mum did not come because she was in the hospital. When we had enough of Gravity, we went to a buffet, the buffet was next to Star City. We had so much fun in Star City and Gravity.

Asma Marjan (9)

Green Crescent Primary School, Basford

A Day Out In The Park

I went to the park with my aunty, mum and my sister. I went on the swings with my sister. My mum was talking to my aunt while she was pushing Hannah on the swing. Then I went on the biggest swing and my aunty was pushing me high. Then we dropped Aunty off at home.

Later, we went to visit Dadema. Me and Hannah played with the kittens. We had a nice meal, we watched TV. It was getting late, we went home. We got ready for bed and brushed our teeth and got our PJs on. Good night.

Safa Chughtai (7)

Green Crescent Primary School, Basford

My New Powers

Dear Diary,

Today I went to Wollaton Hall. It was so amazing and cool but the best thing was that I touched Spider-Man's mask. I was the first person to touch the mask. It was hard and cold. When I touched it, I shot a fireball out my mouth.

I saw a monster and I punched it and then it smashed me into the wall. I punched it with my super speed and it went to space. I used my powers and went to space and I fought.

Mohammed-Yahya Rasool (8)

Green Crescent Primary School, Basford

World War Two

Dear Diary,

In World War Two, I felt like I was going to win the war but David the manager died because he was eating pizza, fish, and apples. The enemies shot him. He died. I went to his house and someone told me David left me a gift. So I went to get the gift, it was a watch that can make me time travel and can make me go to space and I was sad and crying because David died.

Hussain Saeed (8)

Green Crescent Primary School, Basford

House Upside Down

Dear Diary,
Suddenly, my house went upside down when I was asleep. When I woke up I saw my house was upside down and I called my grandad. I felt afraid and scared. I used my wand and I fixed the problem with a spell. Everything was back to normal and I had cereal for breakfast.

Khadija Javaid (5)
Green Crescent Primary School, Basford

Ramadan Moon

Dear Diary,

I am decorating my house for Ramadan and it will also be my birthday. I am excited. I will fast inshAllah.

When I see the moon then I know it is Ramadan. The next day it is Ramadan. I am happy.

Fatima Zahra Sheikh (5)

Green Crescent Primary School, Basford

In Space

Dear Diary,

I went to space and I turned into a superhero forever and I was happy and I was fighting a bad guy. I won the fight. After, I was missing my family so I went back and I turned back to normal.

Ahmad Qureshi (6)

Green Crescent Primary School, Basford

My Holiday

Dear Diary,

I went to Dubai. I went on holiday. I had ice cream. I lived in a hotel. I had chocolate cake. I felt happy too. I went in a pool and was swimming. I thank my parents for all that they do.

Zunaira Muzaffar (5)

Green Crescent Primary School, Basford

My Trip

Dear Diary,

I am going on a trip to Pakistan and I am celebrating Eid there. I am going to wear my favourite clothes and I am going to eat lots of yummy food. I wish I could invite all my teachers.

Zakariyya Imran (6)

Green Crescent Primary School, Basford

The Ship

Dear Diary,

On Friday I went to the ship. Then the ship was sinking into the water. Then I went out to the ship. Then I found an island. Then I made a home.

Essa Khan (6)

Green Crescent Primary School, Basford

Bubble Factory

Dear Diary,
In the bubble factory there were bubbles everywhere and they were different colours. I popped the bubbles and lots of toys came out.

Eesa Ahmadzai (6)
Green Crescent Primary School, Basford

Planet Bouncy

Dear Diary,

I went to Planet Bounce and Red Kangaroo and I felt happy and it was bouncy. I didn't get tired and I touched the sky.

Yasmin Syam (5)

Green Crescent Primary School, Basford

Superpowers

Dear Diary,
One day I had superpowers.
I saved people and I was strong. I could fly!

Yousuf Ahmeti (5)
Green Crescent Primary School, Basford

The Aching Controller

Dear Diary,

Yesterday evening, my joysticks were really hurting. They were also kinda aching as well. I don't see why this child needs to play FIFA so much. In my opinion, he should stop playing. I think somebody should take it off him.

"What time is dinner?"

This is so annoying, he must have glasses. He's on me every day from four until ten.

"Uhh."

Maybe he'll need a drink soon. Or even better, a snack. At this point, I don't care what he does. Anything will do.

Oh yes, finally this kid is off his Xbox. Hip hip hooray!

Mason Ziwange (10)

Heamoor Community Primary School, Heamoor

I Found A Dragon Egg

Dear Diary,
Something incredible happened today! Would you like to know? In the afternoon, I was reading my book when I heard an explosion! I opened my window and scrambled down the drain pipe. There was smoke coming from the secret garden! I landed on the sun-dried concrete. I stumbled in anticipation towards the tiny gaps. The only entrance. I squeezed my body through the entrance. I tripped and fell on the cold floor. I ran towards the stone pillars, and I saw a beautiful, shiny, scaly egg. It was instantly recognisable. It was an immensely rare dragon egg!

Zethar Savage (11)
Heamoor Community Primary School, Heamoor

What's Under The School?

Dear Diary,

Yesterday, I went to school. When I was at school, I heard an unusual sound under the school.

"What is that?" I said to my teacher.

"I don't know," answered my teacher.

At that point, the clever builders were there and were just about to look under the school so we asked them to see what was under there. When they looked under the school, there was a magic unicorn. We were so surprised and excited because we had never seen a unicorn before. It turns out that the unicorn was left there a hundred years ago.

Libby Cringle (9)

Heamoor Community Primary School, Heamoor

Football Incident

Dear Diary,
Today was the weirdest day of my life. Shall I say what happened? I woke up shivering with my friends inside this crammed bag. I could hear this loud chanting noise. Here they come. Who? You may ask. France and England. Why do they squish me before they beat me up with their feet? Harry Kane stepped up to take the penalty. Wheee! Oh my. I'd smashed through this woman's window. "I can't believe you, Harry Kane, you are so bad. I can't pay for this, I'm so sorry." She couldn't hear me but I was so sorry.

Tyler Dale (10)
Heamoor Community Primary School, Heamoor

The Diary Of The Last Person Alive

Dear Diary,

I've been locked down by myself for weeks! There's been a zombie apocalypse and I don't want to die, so I stayed down in the basement. It started to get cold and damp and it smelled! So I decided to go out, and I prayed that it was done. It was but there was nobody there. Cars and buildings were broken. I was horrified! There were bodies all over the floor. I cried and cried when I heard a voice say softly, "Don't cry." I looked behind me and saw an angel. "You're going to Heaven now."

Elsie Searle (9)

Heamoor Community Primary School, Heamoor

The Diary Of A Phone

Dear Diary,
Today I was rapidly pulled off my charger. And then I got poked in the face by some acrylic nails. I was slipped into the back pocket ready to begin the day. When it was breakfast time, I got some annoying pings, rings and a please leave me alone message after the tone. I was tapped in the face by greasy butter fingers, then got a splash of water in my face. Ah! So annoying. I was tapped four times for a password and clicked on FaceTime. FaceTime's the best, there's no touching your face till the end.

Aimee Maddern (10)
Heamoor Community Primary School, Heamoor

The Mermaid That Goes On Adventures

Dear Diary,

Today I was swimming through the ocean when I felt like I wanted an adventure. First, I went to the creepy cave, where there was a monster that screamed at me and it was so scary.

I shouted, "Help me, there is a monster after me!" Then a seahorse arrived and helped me.

Secondly, I went to the surface. When I went up there, a bird flew past and squawked at me, and then a dolphin helped me and took me down to my home to help me get safe.

"Thank you for your help!" I said.

Willow Trevail (9)

Heamoor Community Primary School, Heamoor

Alexander The Great

Dear Diary,

It all started when a soldier came over to me with a knife in his stomach! I knew what I had to do. I put on my armour and ran outside... I then saw thousands of Persians. I quickly killed some and got to work protecting my soldiers and king. The Greeks joined the battle and killed most of the Persians. We caught some and interrogated them; they told us about their plan. We ran into the next field and saw the most terrifying thing - lightning struck and thunder roared and colour illuminated the ground.

Alexander Davy Eddy (11)

Heamoor Community Primary School, Heamoor

Tails' Diary

Dear Diary,

These have been the most exciting days ever. I was bullied by people and they were pulling my extra tail. Then a blue blur knocked them out. I followed it to thank them and they invited me to help them defeat Eggman. I agreed and we set off. We got to a chemical plant and I had to carry Sonic (that's his name) because there were rising chemicals. When we left, he had to spit out chemicals. We found Eggman, he was in a drill driving at us. He defeated him and released the stickies he used evilly.

William Perry (11)
Heamoor Community Primary School, Heamoor

Da Fishy

Dear Diary,

Today was a stressful day for a fishy. Should I say what happened? So, first, it was a peaceful day when dun dun dun! The naughty fishers caught me. They had food fit for the fishy king, so I thought it wouldn't hurt to have some... I was in a net - my friends were horrified. I was the favourite fishy! I had to escape, and fast! I tried a fishy dance to distract, but it failed. But then I realised... I was small enough to fit through the holes! So, I slipped through and back into the pond!

Lois Murrish (10)

Heamoor Community Primary School, Heamoor

Mario And Cappy

Dear Diary,

Me and Cappy went to Mushroom Village to Mushroom Land. Me and Cappy left Mushroom Village and went to Odyssey Land to get an Odyssey. But we needed moons. We had to fight. Later to get a moon I had a horrendous fight and got a moon and put it in the Odyssey. I got out of there and headed to Metro Kingdom and had to fight Tonks and fight the centipede. I defeated the centipede and got his moon. We went to the moon to defeat Bowser. We found Bowser and defeated Bowser and grabbed his moon.

Jason Ward (10)

Heamoor Community Primary School, Heamoor

My Life As An IPad

Dear Diary,

My life is the worst life ever! I've been cracked, smashed and had grease and slimy stuff all over me. I have been cleaned though, I have been all sorts of colours and I have a long time. But if my owner isn't careful, it will be expensive to fix. I am very smart, my owner can ask me anything and I will be correct. I die and come back to life. Plug me in and I'll be alright. I have a very good memory, better than you. Lots of people play on me and play with me.

Emilie Marshall (10)

Heamoor Community Primary School, Heamoor

The Tennis Racket

Dear Diary,

I was sleeping at 10:30am because it was my day off but a human picked me up. His big hands on my handle, he bashed me on a ball for one hour. He left me on the floor for another human. Someone else came along and bashed me on the ball for three hours. Four hours in total. I was tired from all the bashing. And I got left on the floor until 12am. Until someone found me and put me back with my friends. I couldn't sleep all night because I heard other humans playing.

Caleb Turner (10)

Heamoor Community Primary School, Heamoor

The Life Of A Cookie

Dear Diary,

The last couple of weeks have been crazy. It started when me and my friend were lying in a pack of cookies. When I was in the middle of a conversation I started to feel weird. It was a person shaking us. I heard a beeping noise. A couple of seconds later, I was in a car. When we got home, one of my friends was being stepped on. I was really sad. I was left in a cupboard. It was uncomfortable. A week later, I was taken out of the cupboard. I was a weird green colour.

Scarlett Corin (9)

Heamoor Community Primary School, Heamoor

The Magical School And The Magic Kids

Dear Diary,
Today I went to school. I did my normal stuff and the fire alarm went off. I had no cardigan or coat, I was freezing. I had to leave my lunch but that's not the important part. One kid, it was me. I sank the school underwater. OMG, I can't believe it was me. Then the school turned into a talking house and then turned into a ship, a pirate ship. Wow. I screamed. I had levitating powers. OMG, all my friends had powers. I lifted my friend. The school was magic!

Lily Bawden-Bonell (8)
Heamoor Community Primary School, Heamoor

A Day At The Shop

Dear Diary,
Today I snuck out of my house to go to the shop.
The shop I am going to is Sainsbury's. When I got
to the shop and went inside, everyone I walked
past probably thought, *What? A cat in a shop?*
I decided to walk down the cat food aisle. Then I
remembered the humans at home so I did a little
bit of marking and left the shop. I will go to the
shop again next month. When I got home, the
humans gave me lots of treats and then I went to
sleep in my bed.

Daisy Coates (8)

Heamoor Community Primary School, Heamoor

Sonic's Diary

Dear Diary,
I was just chilling around in Green Hill when suddenly I heard an explosion! I went to go check it out and no surprise, Eggman was up to no good. I went to go confront him but then a portal appeared and sucked me into a new world! Everything looked so futuristic. Then I saw a path so I went down it. After that, I fell into some ooze. I got out quickly though. After all that, it was boring going to all these worlds but then I saw Eggman and stopped him.

Archie Praed (10)
Heamoor Community Primary School, Heamoor

The Magical Treasure Hunt

Diary Diary,
One day, there was a little girl called Isabell, me. I was in my garden and in a little clock was a map. But it wasn't an ordinary map, it was a magical map. I was so excited! I looked at the map, it was amazing. So it led to a magical forest. So I packed my stuff and went. I walked past a river and there was the magical forest. I went in. I searched for hours. I finally found it! I was so excited. I looked at the map. I opened it, it had a crown.

Halle Hawkes (9)

Heamoor Community Primary School, Heamoor

The Life Of An Office Printer

Dear Diary,

Humans are creatures, they use me and refill me when I don't need it. It feels like I have been wheeled around the world and back again. They hurt me and press me when they think I am broken. I am fed up of this! It needs to stop. Hang on a minute, I can't because how are they going to print stuff? They will replace me. I can't stop. I will only work six days a week and on Sunday I can shut myself down. That is printer life for you.

Bonnie Richards (9)

Heamoor Community Primary School, Heamoor

Wall

Dear Diary,

Today was the worst day ever because I had big stuff stuck on me. It was so annoying. I got kicked by a kid. I also had to see people do their shopping. Being a wall is so boring. I'm so angry! I bet you had a better day than me. I wish I could be more of a fun object like a tennis ball. There is no positive in being a wall. It is so boring. I get to stay for a hundred years until I get knocked down. That will be the end of my life.

Jasmine Wright (10)

Heamoor Community Primary School, Heamoor

Diary Of A Football

Dear Diary,
Today has been painful! I have been kicked by things with hair, been kicked into a thing with holes, stamped on then at lunch I got stood on again by smaller things with hair and OMG I've been stamped on again! Why? Why? Oh yeah, so I got put in a box and kicked into a tree (felt dizzy) came back down, got stuck in a pile of mud, came out of the box and poked with a stick and with a pole. Be back tomorrow hopefully.

Isla-Grace Walker (10)
Heamoor Community Primary School, Heamoor

The Dimension Bike Disaster

Dear Diary,

Today I bought a new time travel hover bike. I started to go to different dimensions. I time travelled to a scary and terrifying dimension and got lost. Then I got worried and scared and I said, "Where am I?"

Then I said, "I think I am in the underworld!"

It was scary in the underworld. So I went back home. Then I reunited with my mum and dad. So we went for a walk.

Arlo Jack Morrison Andrews (9)

Heamoor Community Primary School, Heamoor

The Duel Between Harry And Voldemort

Dear Diary,

Yesterday was a very tough day because I saw Harry Potter outside Hogwarts School of Witchcraft and Wizardry duelling with Voldemort. The second I heard Voldemort say, "Avada Kedavra!" I ran into the scene, took out my wand and shouted, "Protego!"

The killing spell reflected off the shield charm. Then it was Harry's turn. He shouted, "Expelliarmus!" Sadly, the spell missed by inches. Before I could make another spell, Voldemort said, "Crucio!" Harry wriggled around in pain.

I said, "Crucio!" back.

The pain didn't last long. Soon the pain in Harry was over. Voldemort disappeared so we won.

Alp Kilic (8)

Honeywell Junior School, Wandsworth

The Future Warning

I woke up to discover a girl staring at me. It was creepy, like I was looking at my reflection but messy. She mouthed, "Help!" then dashed away. I chased after her.

"Wait!" I screamed.

"I can't, I'm your future!" she screeched.

Before my eyes, she disappeared. I stood there speechless. I looked at the floor and saw three notes that I'd never seen before.

The first said, 'Evacuate'.

The second said, 'Earth collapsed'.

The last one said, 'Space'.

I almost fainted. I rushed down to tell them everything. After explaining, the floor started to shake. Is this the end?

Charlotte Del Serra (9)
Honeywell Junior School, Wandsworth

Heroes

One lovely day, me and my friends were having a stroll in the dark park. Suddenly, I turned around in shock and found Shaun and Gromit running.
"What happened?" I said.
They shrugged. They felt something touching them.
Then, I said, "Why are you so... Guys?" I said, "I think they were kidnapped." I said worriedly, "Help!" But no one was there. I saw a pitch-black hole.
"Guys! I'm coming!"
I saw Gromit, Shaun and my intimidated friends. Finally, I said a spell and my friends were free! I hugged them strongly and we flew up together.

Olivia Fucci (8)
Honeywell Junior School, Wandsworth

Major Kim Beake's Mission

Dear Diary,

Flying has always been my dream, and today that dream came true. I was born with wings that seemed too small to ever let me leave the ground. I felt banished from the thrilling world outside my home pond but never gave up hope.

After years of arduous, captivating work, I built a jet pack. When my flock was asleep, I set off for space! Soon the pond became distant, then Earth itself. I hit the thermosphere, which glowed fluorescent orange, before entering the International Space Station. Mission accomplished!

Signed,

Kim Beake... The one and only astroduck.

Savithri Grunert (10)

Honeywell Junior School, Wandsworth

Life Of John Cena

After a long day of wrestling, I broke my arm trying to fight the wrestler Brawler. Everyone was disappointed in me, so I decided I'd get revenge on Brawler. A few weeks later, when I was out of the hospital, I went to the WWE and to my astonishment, Brawler was waiting for me in the ring. A colossal crowd was chanting my name.

"John Cena! John Cena!"

And only a measly crowd was cheering, "Brawler! Brawler!"

Aggressively, I charged at Brawler and knocked him out cold. When he got back up, the referee announced, "And the winner is... Cena!"

Luca Amati (8)

Honeywell Junior School, Wandsworth

The Worst Day Of School

Dear Diary,
My name is Amelia Moneysworth. Today has been the worst day ever! Today at school, everybody was teasing me because I was born without my left arm. The school bully called me Armless Amelia every time she saw me. I've told her to stop but she never listens. All she says is, "If you're so 'money's worth', buy yourself a prosthetic arm."
So I told my parents and they said, "Don't listen to her. Stand up to her."
So I did.
I said, "Does it make you feel good to make me feel bad?"
Then I walked away.

Deniz Odemis (9)
Honeywell Junior School, Wandsworth

Voiceless

Dear Diary,

Alright, before I start rambling self-consciously, I'm not writing because I want to, but because Mum explained that if I ever want to see the light of the sun, I must write in this bothersome diary! Honestly, I wish that I could make them understand that I'm human, despite my differences! Since birth, my body has lacked pigment. The only colour in my persona is my startlingly bright emerald eyes. This genetic condition makes me an albino. Here at the lab, I feel so voiceless! I'll rant more when I escape these tedious observations. Love, Lea.

Alia Bounouara (11)

Honeywell Junior School, Wandsworth

Blue-52 (The Loneliest Whale In The World)

Dear Diary,
Another pod left without warning last night. The calves hadn't adapted to their songs yet and for a while, I thought they could understand bits of mine. My song is fifty-five hertz where it's meant to be thirty-five. The lonely song that only I can hear. The one that's a whole different language to every other whale. The older baleens don't want to have young in their pod that wouldn't be able to communicate with them if in danger. Common sense, really. I just wish it wasn't and that finally, someone would understand my song too.

Evelyn Butler (11)

Honeywell Junior School, Wandsworth

Time Travelling To Victorians

Dear Diary,

Today was when I discovered that I could time travel. It all started when I was having an ordinary day, walking outside on the streets. Suddenly, I stepped on a strange-looking stone, and everything went black. Seconds after, I was in the Victorian times. People were walking around me in stiff black and white dresses. I could see wooden houses and maids wearing aprons. Giddy and nervous, I stared around in confusion when out of the corner of my eye, I spotted a strangely shaped stone. Without thinking, I stepped on it. Everything changed. I was back.

Ania O'Neill (9)

Honeywell Junior School, Wandsworth

01/06/2022's Diary Entry - Mission To Become The Correct Size!

Dear Diary,

Yesterday something extraordinary happened. I woke up and looked at my clock. To my surprise, I found it had grown to the size of a humungous painting! I had shrunk and had turned into a pixie! *Oh no,* I thought, *tomorrow is Monday and I have school!* I suddenly remembered as I am a pixie if I say 'enchantment' I will go to Enchantment Land, so I said, "Enchantment." I found myself outside a stall with ointment for making people bigger so I bought some. I rubbed myself until I got to the right size and returned home.

Florence Cawdron (9)

Honeywell Junior School, Wandsworth

The Mysterious Journey

Dear Diary,

It was a hectic day. Let me go back to the start. So I was peacefully drawing then all of a sudden a big dragon said, "Hop on my back."

So I did.

"Where would you like to go?" said the dragon.

"Australia!"

So off he went up, up and away.

"Would you like to go higher?"

"Yes!"

As he went, the city got smaller and smaller. As I looked up I saw clouds like cotton candy dancing in the air. When I looked around, we were there, it was beautiful! And that's my hectic journey.

Nell Pringle Rogers (8)

Honeywell Junior School, Wandsworth

An Eggstraordinary Chick (Tiny)

As I hatched out of my egg, I looked around me and whispered a little, "Tweet."
My three sisters immediately snuggled around me. I tried to pull a smile on my beak. I was feeling a confetti of feelings all at once: sad, happy, nervous, frightened, excited, calm, warm and fuzzy. Hugging my sisters tighter, enjoying my introduction to the world! After my sisters released me, I fluttered to breakfast. Chomping down on a delicious bowl of cornflakes and washing it down with a cup of milk from Mummy. It was a great start to the day. I was overeggcited!

Stella Packer (7)

Honeywell Junior School, Wandsworth

The Beginning

Today was an amazing day. I was walking in the woods when I came across a pathway bordered by willow trees with gnarled trunks. Something mysterious was happening there. So without much thought, I darted into the trees. I followed the crumbling pathway and emerged to find an unexplored city. It was a myriad of wonders. Abandoned and crumbling but ever so beautiful, with stone archways, lifeless fountains and faded mosaics. I turned to look back at my pathway but it had disappeared. I was so utterly lost yet so at home. It is here, Diary, that I found you.

Francesca Brooke (11)
Honeywell Junior School, Wandsworth

The Incredible Diary Of The Good Kidnapper

Dear Diary,

I've recruited several new agents to help us reclaim our land. Although I am the most wanted person in the South Island, I mean well. The only reason I'm kidnapping Maori children is that I want them to have a good life. They want their land back, they want their identity back. The truth is that Six does hate me, I mean who can blame her? I kidnapped her. But she has become my sidekick! Today, she told me about another potential recruit, then looked into my eyes and said, "I think we're going to be great friends."

Louisa Yelland (10)

Honeywell Junior School, Wandsworth

My Dog Ate My Homework!

Dear Diary,

My dog ate my homework! Quite literally gobbled my geography with glee. I'd finally finished my project on the fjords of the Faroe Islands when I sat back to tuck into my sausage and mash supper. As I bit into my banger, it bounced out my mouth, pinged off my plate and landed in the middle of Lake Sorvagsvtn (the largest lake in the Faroes). In a flash, my mischievous mutt mounted the table and snaffled my sausage along with my assignment. My teacher will never believe me but trust me, and my meddling mongrel, it's true.

Monty Wheeler (9)

Honeywell Junior School, Wandsworth

Bill's Brazen Beach Escape

Dear Diary,

The name is Bill Starling. I was the most fearsome captain, King of the Atlantic Ocean. Following months of sailing the stormy seas, staring at nothing but the deep, dark depths of the briny blue, the crew on The Diamond Grace became mutinous. They strapped a cannon onto my bootstraps. It blasted me high into the sky and then I plunged into the foaming waters. The weight of the waves crashing over me loosened the cannon and I was able to swim to shore. I stood in the shallows, in the distance a ship was sailing towards me...

Imogen Hardy (9)

Honeywell Junior School, Wandsworth

Pushing Into A Magical Painting

Yesterday, Lara and I went on a school trip to the museum. We went to the Egyptian artefacts, got bored and explored the other paintings. A silly boy pushed us into a painting, we saw a note saying, 'Save the village, the king is destroying it!'
We got to the king and demanded him to stop. We were sent down to the dungeon but slipped through a window to see a wizard. He said, "Two magical flowers grant two wishes. The dragon knows you deserve the flowers."
We wished for the town to be safe and got home happily.

Marnie Clark (8)

Honeywell Junior School, Wandsworth

My Teacher's Secret Lair

So yesterday was a normal day and all my classes were fine until it was Mr Sketchy's class. When he walked out, I shouted, "Party time!"
But he heard me and gave me a detention. When I was in detention, I noticed something. I saw Mr Sketchy walk down a staircase. So I followed him down. I saw children were in containers and were changing into aliens and when I looked over at Mr Sketchy he'd turned into an alien with sharp teeth. After that, I jumped out the window screaming over the hills. Now Mr Sketchy is sketchy.

Declan Provino (9)
Honeywell Junior School, Wandsworth

My Teacher Got Angry And Turned Into A Monster

So yesterday was a normal day. I went to my classes and all was fine. Until English class with Miss Firepants. My class was shouting and screaming! The noise was deafening. Miss Firepants was screaming even louder to try to calm down the children. Then in the heat of the moment, Miss Firepants' face went bright red and her nose was smoking with fire! Then a red light showed on her face. Miss Firepants was raised in the air and transformed into a hideous fire-breathing dragon! We all screamed and ran out of the classroom in horror.

Hadley Provino (11)
Honeywell Junior School, Wandsworth

The Rugball Final

Dear Diary,

I've had an amazing day. When I woke up, a smile grew across my face. It was the rugball final. And I was playing. I rushed to the stadium, beating the traffic. When I arrived, the crowds were chanting and I was nervous. In the first half, they thrashed us but in the second we improved drastically. In the closing seconds, we were five points down. The buzzer sounded. It was the last play of the game. I received the ball, sprinted to the try line, placed the ball down and scored the kicking conversion. We won!

Peter Gray (10)
Honeywell Junior School, Wandsworth

A Banana's Life

Dear Diary,

These last twenty-four hours were the worst. It was hell! Somebody came in through a door, picked me up, peeled off my skin and ate me! That, my friends, was it. I was already in agony when my skin got peeled off, so how am I writing this to you if I'm dead you ask me? Well, I'm in heaven. Now, as I write this, I watch my body (I'm a soul/spirit) get eaten, swallowed, digested, dried, shrivelled and stored until *plop! Splash! Bong!* My body is free! But also now it's poop! Until next time!

Ida Cobanoglu (8)
Honeywell Junior School, Wandsworth

When My Friend Turns Into A Chicken

Dear Diary,
Today I went to the zoo of dance. We drank millions of soda cans. After that, we went to the farm. We saw the cows, the chickens, the geese, the pigs, and so on. We bought a pack of eggs and went there.

Dear Diary,
When we finished the sleepover, we took eggs for breakfast. My friend went home still in her pyjamas. Four hours later, the phone rang. I was alone in the house so I took the phone. It was my friend's mum.
She said, "My child is a chicken."
My jaw dropped down.

Charles Dupont (8)
Honeywell Junior School, Wandsworth

When I Escaped School

Dear Diary,

Today wasn't so bad. We had maths... It's boring and difficult. The teacher was droning on. I wanted to dart out of the classroom, run and jump out the windows. I stayed seated but not for long. In five minutes, the bell rang for a break. We scraped our chairs and ran. In the playground, we have a fence. I walked up slowly, checking that the teacher was not looking, jumped over and I escaped. Woo! Of course, you know what happens. I got suspended. I don't have to go to school! Sorry, have to go, bye!

Bluebell Gorden-Malone (10)

Honeywell Junior School, Wandsworth

An Unlikely Friendship

"Ruff!" I barked as a thorn poked into my paw. My owner Gary came rushing over and scooped me up. He looked at my paw and took me straight to the vet.

"Meow!" said a cat as she came out of the vet's room. I took one look at her and I knew I was in trouble.

"The vet is evil, you won't like him," she said. "Run!" So that's exactly what I did. The cat followed me.

"Thank you for warning me," I said. We both ran home as friends and made an animal shelter.

Nia Tainton (8)

Honeywell Junior School, Wandsworth

My Magic Adventure

Dear Diary,

Today I was wandering in the forest and found a magic bag. I looked inside and saw it belonged to the tree demon. I was looking for the demon when I found him. He thought I stole it and he attacked me.

I shouted, "I found it, I didn't steal it!"

He replied, "I'm sorry."

And he got a bottle full of weird liquid and poured it on a tree and there was a pop. In a blink, a treehouse appeared.

The tree demon said, "You can live here." He walked away and now I live there.

Ernie Carter Croucher (8)

Honeywell Junior School, Wandsworth

How To Grow Time

Dear Diary,
Today I crashed my ship and I landed on Earth.
Most of the animals there were friendly and
remembered when my ancestors visited. But the
tall bald ones called humans were shocked by me.
And I was shocked that they had no spare
spaceships to send me home. They laughed when I
asked for a new time drive. (Time travel is a
mystery to them.) Two young humans did not
laugh. They wanted my knowledge. In a forest, I
showed them how to grow time. Soon we will
travel together and they will teach their people.

Alexander Bamber (9)

Honeywell Junior School, Wandsworth

The Super Boy

I was sitting in class and my teacher was talking. Suddenly, my watch rang and I knew it was time for an adventure. As usual, I went to my toilet transporter to get to Chunky Town. When I got there the whole town looked like the messiest child's bedroom. I knew immediately that this was the work of Dr Doom. I looked for some villagers but they all vanished. I knew I was too late. I was worried about the villagers. Where was Dr Doom? I decided tomorrow I would start my search for Dr Doom with my sidekick Boo-Boo.

Selma Yoruk (7)

Honeywell Junior School, Wandsworth

The Girl Who Escaped From A Strict Orphanage

Dear Diary,

I have had a stressful time escaping from an orphanage. It's not just any orphanage, it's like a prison! Most people think it's fun, you play games. No! All you do is learn how to be polite and be better than other "snotty kids" as they call it. I am so tired of it! "Why did my parents leave me here?" I escaped! But I don't really know my way around the UK. It is quite boring if I say so myself. I don't quite know where to go.

Diary time finished.

Afsana Ahmed (9)
Honeywell Junior School, Wandsworth

The Volcano

Looking down at my feet, the molten lava, crimson in colour, started spitting at me. The wooden plank strained to take my weight, and then came some laughter of merciless souls below. My heart pounded as I lunged for a rope. Seconds later, the wooden plank I was on fell into the abyss. Before I switched to another rope, I saw a copious amount of ledges. That was my way out. I leapt onto the ledge and bolted up the spiral stairs and burst out of the volcano like a cheetah. I had done it! I had escaped Mount Doom.

Liam O'Healai (10)
Honeywell Junior School, Wandsworth

The Day That Changed My Life

Dear Diary,
The sun woke me. Gold streamed through my window warming my room and told me things were okay. But when I got to school, the noise seeped inside my brain and people pointed at me. My heart was racing, my head spinning and my mouth was dry. Again, I left the classroom. But there was a new kid there. He had noise cancellers on and seemed nervous like me. I felt the warm sun on my face again and felt courage. I said hi and he replied. The first time that ever happened. Maybe I will try tomorrow.

Alex Ardalan (9)
Honeywell Junior School, Wandsworth

82

Diary Of The Laziest Kid On Earth

Dear Diary,

Nothing very interesting ever happens to me. I'm not the most active kid in my class or you could say Earth. The most exciting thing I've done in ages is when I went to the Royal Academy of Arts yesterday. There was a ginormous wall calling me to scribble on it, so I did (in crazy colours). Then I went to Fortnum and Mason, a very fancy Victorian place which has an ice cream parlour with free toppings! I ordered a gazillion of course. It was fun but now I'm ready to be lazy again.

Idris Weston (8)

Honeywell Junior School, Wandsworth

Bianca The Plant!

Dear Diary,

I am a plant, Bianca the plant. I have a brother called Bobby, a mum named Beatrice, a stepdad called Ben and a step-sister called Bella. Me, my mum and my brother are spider plants but Ben and Bella are aloe veras. I hate the way that humans just buy us for decoration. They just dump us somewhere where people can see us and then don't take any notice of us unless they need to water us. Bobby and me can't even be seen. Our owner just stuffed us behind Jeff and Judy, the cane plants.

Suki Slater (9)

Honeywell Junior School, Wandsworth

The Terror Of Going To Ballet

Dear Diary,

I am terrified of Miss Windy (my ballet teacher). She makes me do the splits and rips up my leotard. She is basically the devil of ballet. Once I did a ballet exam, and she tortured me. I forgot what was fifth position. Most of all, she wouldn't even let me fart, cough or go to the toilet. One day, she had mustard in her bag for dinner but instead, she squirted it at me! Just because she was mad and lost her temper. P.S. Mustard is my worst topping for food! I felt sorry for Miss Windy.

Sophie Dempster (8)

Honeywell Junior School, Wandsworth

A Monster Day

Dear Diary,
It started like any ordinary day. But today was a little crazy when I turned Mrs Ince into a monster! I secretly knew I had superpowers but I had never used them before. I was concentrating way too hard on my maths when *poof!* Smoke was everywhere. I felt guilty at first but it worked out brilliantly as Mrs Ince has always wanted to be a monster. She made lots of new monster friends in the staffroom and was a super friendly monster teacher to her pupils. So it ended up being great.

Georgia Freud (8)
Honeywell Junior School, Wandsworth

Zooming Through Space

Dear Diary,

How exhausting today has been! It all started when Dad called us for bedtime. But my siblings and I were much too energetic to sleep. We decided to explore beyond the house. We were going flying! We weaved in and out of the stars. How funny it was to see the galactic neighbours moaning about our whooshing engines. I loved zooming between Saturn and Mars but the night was washing over us. It was time to shoot back home. How relieved we were to see our starry beds. I fell asleep immediately.

Elodie Sack (9)

Honeywell Junior School, Wandsworth

The Great Fire Of London

Dear Diary,

I am currently trapped in a disastrous situation. Let me tell you from the start. It was late on the first of September 1666, when I was baking bread for my final customer. While the bread was baking, I drifted off into a deep sleep. A couple of hours had passed when I was woken by an appalling smell of smoke. I rushed downstairs to find that my kitchen was on fire. I ran to get some water but when I returned it was too late... I had started The Great Fire of London! Thomas Farriner.

Penny Mountford (10)

Honeywell Junior School, Wandsworth

The Magic Pencil At School

Dear Diary,

My day was like no other. As I was getting out my pencil case at school, my pencil flew out! I picked it up and started drawing. But I let go of the pencil because it knew exactly what I wanted to draw! I sat there, baffled. Friends came over and looked at my drawing. One said, "Wow, I love that drawing! Can you draw a 3D shape?"

So I drew a 3D shape in the air and guess what? A shape of a robot's hand came out and that's the day I decided to be an engineer.

Benjamin Chubb (8)

Honeywell Junior School, Wandsworth

The Adventure Of Milly The Cat

When I woke up, it was a sunny day. I thought it would be a nice day to play in the garden. I came to the tip of my treehouse and jumped down, knowing cats always land on their feet. I didn't stay in the garden. I wandered off into the city. I saw a girl looking at me. She picked me up and brought me to her home. When she got there, she asked her mum if they could keep me.

Mum said, "We'll decide tomorrow."

When everyone was asleep, I jumped out the window into the darkness.

Lara Ostroumoff (8)

Honeywell Junior School, Wandsworth

A Ladybug Called Hope

The lockdown was no fun, it felt like I was trapped in a cage and I couldn't stretch out to the nature beyond me.

I kept asking, "When can I go outside? I want to go!"

One day, when I was humming a tune, I felt so bored of lying on the bed that I fell asleep! I dreamed of playing with my friends, going to school and seeing teachers welcoming me with happy smiles. Although, something was missing. I opened my eyes, and out of the window came a little ladybug and her name was Hope.

Julia Mammadova (10)

Honeywell Junior School, Wandsworth

Raina's First Swimming Lesson

Dear Diary,

A few weeks ago, I went to my first swimming lesson with no one that I knew. I was really scared and afraid and was really shy when Mr Lakeonder asked me to show how to do a front stroke to everyone. I told him I didn't want to but all he said was, "Don't be afraid and believe in yourself."

So I tried to believe in myself and it actually worked! Soon enough, after loads of hard work, we had to go home. Now, these days, I achieve more by believing in myself.

Bianca Vecchi (9)

Honeywell Junior School, Wandsworth

A Disastrous Birthday

Dear Diary,

This was the worst day ever! Today I turned eight years old. I woke up to find an enormous box! I ran towards it. It was in the kitchen. Little did I know that inside were broken jars of pickle juice. When I opened it, I got soaked head to toe! I went to wash but when I turned on the water, disgusting green goo replaced it! I turned off the shower and headed towards Mum's room. When I looked, she wasn't there! I realised it was school time and I had to go there now.

Arvin Kaygisiz (8)
Honeywell Junior School, Wandsworth

My Amazing Birthday

Dear Diary,

This birthday I had the best birthday ever. So I went to Spain with my family and they surprised me by going to the Spanish Olympics. As a bigger surprise, I got to see my favourite gymnast Sofie Gastro from Brazil. And it got better. I got a private lesson. I squealed. I felt like a star. I felt famous. I could scream. It was the best thing in my life. All my sad feelings had gone away. It was too good to be true but it was. And my family ate hot dogs for our yummy lunch.

Charis Lalobo (9)
Honeywell Junior School, Wandsworth

Brawl Stars Adventure

Dear Diary,

Today was the best day of my life. I was playing Brawl Stars in my room. Then suddenly the phone began to light up. Then before I knew it, I found myself standing in a gigantic box. After work, I saw my high-ranked brawler Edgar and finally understood I was in the video game Brawl Stars. I got very excited and checked if I had any powers, and I did. I had a water blaster so I played and played until I got tired and I noticed a button on my hand. I pressed it and went home.

Tuna Chakat (9)

Honeywell Junior School, Wandsworth

The Forest

Dear Diary,
I had the most unbelievable adventure! My family and I went to a forest in Hawaii. It had fresh flowers and humongous trees. As I entered, my heart was dancing with joy, I felt free! I zoomed off as fast as a cheetah, with arms out stretched touching exotic plants. I stopped in a beam of glittering light. But when the light faded, everything melted around me like I was falling into a black hole. My family was nowhere to be seen... I woke up screaming, sweating and crying.

Aya Sophie Lim (10)
Honeywell Junior School, Wandsworth

The Incredible Diary Of The Dalmatian

Dear Diary,

Today was a very big and hard day. It started. I was lying in bed and I fell asleep then woke back up again. I was tired. It was coming up to 12:30. Then I started eating dog food. I wanted to go to the park which was full of nature. So I barked so the owner knew where I wanted to go. I went to the park and then I went on holiday. I didn't know what we were going to do there, so I barked, barked. *Bark! Bark! Bark! Bark! Bark!*
My owner didn't like it.

George Woolston (7)
Honeywell Junior School, Wandsworth

I Turned My Dog Into A Monster

Dear Diary,

Today I was playing outside with my friends, but I accidentally fell over. I quickly came home like an injured cheetah. When I came back home, Mum told me I was clumsy. Even though I knew it was true, I was angry. When I went into my room, I was so angry I accidentally turned my dog into a monster. He barged out of the room and started attacking the city. But he just would not attack me. I tickled his belly and he came back to a normal dog. After that, Mum said sorry.

Sophie Tolmunen (9)

Honeywell Junior School, Wandsworth

The Day My Life Changed Forever

I woke up this morning to find a slug on my bed. I reached out to grab him. I squeezed him to my chest. Suddenly, Jeffrey licked me. Jeffrey is what I named him. I went to the bathroom, I saw that I had Jeffrey's eyes. I ran downstairs to see Mum who obviously rushed me to A&E. She explained that I had to see a doctor. The doctor told us he couldn't do anything but I had to eat salad at least once in every meal. Yuck! But, I did. And that's how my life changed forever.

Josephine Vannier (9)
Honeywell Junior School, Wandsworth

The Fluffy Cloud City With No Colours

Dear Diary,

Yesterday I went to the fluffy cloud city. I went there because some of the villagers were asking for help. There was not so much time so I went straight away! I went on a flower, not just a flower but a ginormous one. After that, I landed on the city, I saw no colours.

The fairy said, "If you go to the black city, then you will see all the colours. If you take them then they will go back to us."

So we went to the black city and caught all the colours!

Liza Dyshlyuk (8)

Honeywell Junior School, Wandsworth

The Day I Went To Space

It all started when I was at school and I looked out the window. I saw a spaceship landing in the playground. I was over the moon.
Miss Hodgson said, "Everybody, let's go outside and meet the astronauts."
I went outside and rushed inside the spaceship. Without realising it I pressed a button and it turned on and launched into the sky. I was confused and excited at the same time. It was amazing to see the Earth behind me in the galaxy. I was living in my dream.

Elisabeth Petova (8)
Honeywell Junior School, Wandsworth

The Story About My Teddy

I met Brownie in Peter Jones. She was cute and fluffy. I loved her at first sight. I took it home with me on the bus. I was so happy! I took her everywhere! Sadly, I lost her on the 344. I was so sad. My parents called TFL but nobody saw her. One day, I looked on Peter Jones's website and I found her! I was so happy I couldn't contain my excitement. I went immediately to pick her up. We have been BFFs since then. Next Christmas I got a big bear. Then they became best friends.

Antia Corrales (9)
Honeywell Junior School, Wandsworth

Maisie And Her Sea Adventure

Today I had the most exciting day under the sea! Firstly, I went to the beach to collect seashells. I picked up a beautiful shell. I really wanted to be able to breathe underwater. The magical shell turned me into a fish. Between the rocks I spotted a shark. I panicked. I swam but the shark was faster. He was about to eat me when I realised I was too close to shore for the shark to swim. Luckily, I saw the beautiful shell again. I wished to be a human and it came true. I ran home.

Emilia Ostroumoff (8)
Honeywell Junior School, Wandsworth

Kidnapped Then Rescued

Today I went on the most dramatic journey of my life, to creepy Creaky Alley. The creepiest place on Planet Earth. At the darkest part of the alleyway, I felt a bag being pulled over my head and I was dragged into a rusty old car. We were driving for miles before the car screeched to a halt. I heard the sound of children saying, "Thank you."
So I started shouting for help. I saw the lollipop lady from my school whacking the kidnapper over the head with her stick.

Ottilie Taylor Goldsmith (7)

Honeywell Junior School, Wandsworth

My Awesome Day

Dear Diary,

Today was the best. This morning was normal and randomly I was in the middle of my lesson when the deputy head called me out to speak to her. I thought I was in trouble but she said I wasn't. It was awesome. She told me I was chosen from my class to get a year award which was going to a trampoline park. I also got to go to a professional parkour training lesson. I was so excited and was going to go tell my friends about the talk with the deputy head.

Latifa Mursal (9)

Honeywell Junior School, Wandsworth

 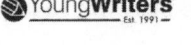

Crazy Day At The Beach

The craziest thing happened today. I thought it was going to be a normal day at the beach. I got bitten by a crab! It was so painful! It only happened because I thought I saw a fin and ran to tell I didn't see the crab! As my mum bandaged my foot, I told her about the fin. We turned around and saw it again. Mum said it couldn't be a shark, maybe it is a dolphin and we went to investigate. We were right. He was super cute and friendly. I didn't want to leave.

Maggie Lumsdon (8)

Honeywell Junior School, Wandsworth

The Incredible Diary Of Santa

Dear Diary,

Ho ho ho ho ho! I dropped all presents off at that point, it was the last house.

"We've been through so many reindeer. Yes you can, Rudolph, but we still have one last house, it's Poppy's abode in the UK."

We put all the presents down but we woke them up! We left as quick as a flash and as we left like I always do, I did a big, "Ho ho ho!"

They were so surprised but now we need to get ready for next Christmas.

Poppy Probert (9)

Honeywell Junior School, Wandsworth

Top Love

Dear Diary,

My name is Helena and I am 10 years old. I like going shopping. One day, I went to the swimming pool. My swimming teacher was very kind, she helped me and I got rewards if I did it. I felt very happy on that day. One day, the teacher brought a dog to swim with me. I was jumping and screaming with joy! I have never touched a dog. The dog was very big and soft. My swimming teacher said that if I did a trick... I did it! I got the dog. I love everyone.

Sara Garcia Ciolczyk (9)

Honeywell Junior School, Wandsworth

My Underwater Trip

Dear Diary,

I was swimming in the sea and I was dragged to the very bottom and I passed out. When I woke up, I had a long tail then I realised I was a mermaid. I first saw some fish, then I wondered how I could breathe underwater. I remembered I was a mermaid. It was really hard to remember. Then I played with other mermaids. I had the best day ever. At the end of the day, I sat on a rock and fell asleep and woke up as a human the next day. I loved that day.

Diana Springs (8)

Honeywell Junior School, Wandsworth

The Cookie

Dear Diary,

I am going to show you my adventure. I am first picked up from a packet and taken to a dark cave and that's where I start my story. Crunched up into a little ball and down the throat, then I begin going through a long tube and begin to be wet and soggy. I'm going down into the stomach and then out into the toilet and I become poo. That's the end of my story, I hope you like it. I am still going through the tubes of the toilet.

Micah Croll-Mensah (9)

Honeywell Junior School, Wandsworth

The Superheroes

Dear Diary,

Today I had to deal with a bank robbery. I used my super strength, then my wife stretched to save some people that were on a bridge. Next one of my super kind kids ran around the robber with his super speed. After that one of my other very kind kids shielded us from an explosion with her force field.

We wear red, yellow and black suits and we have a friend called Frozone, who has ice powers.

Who are we...?

Tate Patterson-Waugh (9)
Honeywell Junior School, Wandsworth

I Got The Superpower To Teleport

I went cave exploring then I saw a glowing stone. It was blue. I touched it. I felt magical. Then my brain told me I had superpowers and said if I say I want to go anywhere it will bring me. I would never be late for school ever again. So I was in school and teleported to the lunch hall. Then the other kids saw that I could teleport then they told Ms Kaden the headteacher and I got suspended. So I joined a superpower school.

Hashim Ahmed (9)

Honeywell Junior School, Wandsworth

My First Archery Competition

I woke up in the morning and packed my bow. I was very excited because it was my first archery competition. I put my bow in the car and got in. We drove ninety minutes to Essex. Finally, we got there and set up my bow. I waited till the assembly started and listened to the judges explaining the rules. Finally, I got to shoot. I shot for a few hours until it was the medal ceremony. I won a gold medal and went home.

Sebastian Radosz (9)

Honeywell Junior School, Wandsworth

Paddington's Adventures

Dear Diary,

Today is my first day in New York. Today I am going to meet my best friend Curious George. He is going to show me around New York. First, we are going to take a train to take a boat to the Statue of Liberty. Then we are going to climb up. Then we are going to climb into a hot air balloon. I got in and my best friend Piggy was there and Curious George waved us away.

From Paddington.

Maddie Pretto (9)

Honeywell Junior School, Wandsworth

Messi's Life

Hello, my name is Messi and I like to play football. I do funny videos too. I like to have fun and go on roller coasters. I also practise in my house, in parks, my house too. Yes, I did say house two times. It is because I practise in my house more than in the parks. Not that much but hey, I did win the 2022 World Cup. I was so happy that I won.

Erick Fereira Sagredo (8)
Honeywell Junior School, Wandsworth

HP's Diary One

Dear Diary,

I never knew I'd have to go and defeat Professor Quirrell. All the time I thought Professor Snape was behind all of this madness. I'm in the hospital with my two friends, Hermione Granger and Ron Weasley. Professor Dumbledore (the headmaster) had just left the room. I thought that Gryffindor had lost the points cup when suddenly we got one hundred and seventy points. We all cheered like mad. Later that day, Uncle Vernon came to pick me up from King's Cross Station and looked very glum because he was picking me up from my very bad "home".

Maximilian Dettlaff (9)

Riverside Community Primary School, St Budeaux

War Child

Dear Diary,
I have the most dreadful news! The war has not ceased. In fact, it seems to have gotten worse. Our house was bombed yesterday; it was terrible, Diary! Smoke and flames engulfed the house. Luckily we escaped. However, Father told me that we must go to live in Oswestry with Aunt Mary. I don't have anything against the village or Aunt Mary but I will miss my school friends. I do hope they survived the bombing. Who knows, maybe I'll even meet some of them in Oswestry. I'm glad to have you Diary, goodnight.
Carolyn Steward 1941.

Liliana Strzelczak (10)
Riverside Community Primary School, St Budeaux

The Boy Who Discovered He Had Magic

Dear Diary,

Today I discovered that I have a magic power! As I was mucking about with an ancient sword, (I'm sixteen, don't worry parents if you are reading this!) it started to glow! Then, despite being rusty, when I swung it at stuff (I know, irresponsible right?) the sword sliced straight through it! It was a magic sword! About my power, it is an all-of-the-elements power, meaning I can control air, water, fire and earth. So if a natural disaster hits anytime soon, you can blame me! I'll be back, and see you next time, Diary.

Jacob Guichard (9)

Riverside Community Primary School, St Budeaux

The RAF's Peaceful Discovery

Dear Diary,

Today something weird happened. It started with a dogfight above the Atlantic. My Spitfire was badly damaged so I hid in the clouds. When I got up there, I discovered a dimension called the Peace Dimension where there are no wars. The residents of this place fixed my plane. Then I met the leader, Chieftain Mark. He told me that soldiers like to retreat here so I found out I didn't discover this dimension. Then I heard a bang and I saw the Germans and obviously they wanted to take over. I'll keep you updated, bye.

Logan Monk (10)

Riverside Community Primary School, St Budeaux

Aliens Vs Humans

Dear Diary,
I live in London. I love it here. Last night when I went to sleep I felt myself flying away. I thought it was a dream. When I woke up, I saw a blue blob with ten eyes that moved to reveal two kind-looking aliens. They smiled and told me their names were Berg and Borg. But, despite making me feel happy, their faces turned sad. They took me by the arms to their boss. Even though I was kicking and screaming, I couldn't help being taken away. I was broken inside. It was a huge tragedy.

Melissa Rowe (10)
Riverside Community Primary School, St Budeaux

The Aquarium Adventure

Dear Diary,

Today I went to an aquarium with my friends. We approached the sharks in the tanks, one was specifically following us. So we aimed a torch at the opposite tank and the reflection hit the shark's eye.

"It left us!" we shouted until...

It was back with its whole family. So we had fun with another shark which by the looks of it, wasn't having fun. So we counted to three and we threw rocks at the tanks and *boom!* The glass shattered and the sharks escaped! Moral - don't be panicked in difficult situations in your life.

Aliyah Kamal (10)
Sacred Heart RC Primary School, Blackburn

Orion

Dear Diary,

You won't believe what happened to me. Let me explain. I am from Planet Endraysea, I was working for the Corrie. I discovered something astonishing. I found the silver key and the morpher. It belonged to the Rangers.

But then the Armada attacked and Endraysea was obliterated. I then morphed. I then learned how to survive. I then destroyed the Armada ship. I then repaired it, which was pretty assiduous. When I went to Earth, I met more Rangers. They were called Troy, Gia, Jake, Emma and Noah. And that's the story of me becoming a Ranger.

Usman Asad (10)

Sacred Heart RC Primary School, Blackburn

Amber Wilton

Sunlight coming through the window, I got up to enjoy the fresh air then suddenly... I heard footsteps. I peeked to see what was there. I saw two rather tall and large figures passing by. I shouted, "Good day!"

Without a word, one of them lent their hand to climb and I did. They introduced themselves as Starnight and Gushstiel, they needed help to defeat their enemy. I should open my imagination to fight till the battle was over.

We won. Then a big bright light shone on my face. I was on my bed again! It was amazing.

Shanelle Ofosu (10)
Sacred Heart RC Primary School, Blackburn

The Golden Web

Dear Diary,

Today I awoke to a crisp spring morning. I went to the cook to ask what was for breakfast but she said we were out of strawberries. They're my favourite food! So I insisted on going to the garden and getting some. My friends Kaylie, Ethel and Angela went too. As we were walking, my friend Angela wasn't looking as she broke a web. The spider was angry so I went to the dresser and took some golden string. I spent almost an hour making a new web. The lesson for today is that you must have patience.

Abeeha Naheed (9)

Sacred Heart RC Primary School, Blackburn

The Dragon Who Met A Lion

There was a creature school that was very popular. I, the dragon, was always lonely and no one wanted to play with me. I always got bullied. One day, it was my birthday and one of my wishes was to have a nice friend. The next day a new creature joined the school called Alex the lion. I helped him settle into the school and we soon became very good friends. I was praised by my teachers for showing kindness to my new classmate. I started to enjoy coming to school more often. I love you, my dearest Alex.

Amaya (9)
Sacred Heart RC Primary School, Blackburn

The Day At The Park

Dear Diary,
On a sunny morning, I realised I hadn't taken my cute dog for a walk. I felt bad so I put my coat on and off we went to the enjoyable park. Me and my dog were craving ice cream so we gladly went to the colossal ice cream van. The ice cream man was nice. He gave me my favourite ice cream which was a double chocolate scoop with bubblegum sauce and a chocolate flake to top it off. I felt miserable for my dog. So I treated her with a nice refreshing bottle of mineral water.

Huria Naveed (9)
Sacred Heart RC Primary School, Blackburn

The Scary Trip Dream

One day we had a letter from school about a Blackpool trip and my mum said, "If you want you can go."
So I said, "Okay," then I paid for it.
On the trip day we all sat on the coach and we were there. At first I felt so excited and then I felt someone call me. When I looked back a witch was staring at me. I was so scared. So the witch had a knife in her hand and tried to kill me but then I screamed. It was a dream.

Hamna Arooj (9)
Sacred Heart RC Primary School, Blackburn

Magic Powers

Billy the monster, who wasn't a scary one, went to monster school. He was supposed to be working but he loved his diary. He wrote what his day was like and what he played with his friends. But one day he couldn't say what happened because he had such a bad day! He didn't know what to do but all he knew was to look in his diary and find the page that said 'Magic Powers'. So he looked and he said, "Make me have a good day."
And suddenly it was a great day and it was like magic.

Mia Clark (8)
Spring Cottage Primary School, Hull

Stitch's Diary

Dear Diary,

I am Stitch. You may think I have an easy life with Lilo. But no, I have to go out every day and you might be thinking well won't you like fresh air? Well, Lilo drags me around. And her mean friends call me a monster. I mean come on. I might be a little crazy but I'm still nice. So later, I might get better at looking good for her friends. Thanks for looking at my diary.

Stitch.

Aoife Dodd (7)
Spring Cottage Primary School, Hull

School Diary

It was my first day of school and I wanted to make friends but this is the story of what happened. I went down the stairs, I was very worried but I was very scared as well but I don't know what to do. I ran. I was scared so I ran some more. What to do? There was another new kid just like me. Friends forever together, never apart. I hope we are always friends.

Ellie Todd (8)
Spring Cottage Primary School, Hull

R2D2's Amazing Adventure

I was very bored and had nothing to do. So I went to a random desert and found this apple. It wasn't just any old apple! So I ate it and up! Up! Up! And away. I randomly got sent up into space. I didn't know it was an enchanted apple.

Up in space, I was wondering how to get back to Earth. I finally went back to Earth! Bye.

Me, R2D2.

Matilda Rennard (8)

Spring Cottage Primary School, Hull

A Day In The Life Of Superman

I wear a red and blue costume. I have to fly really fast through the dangerous cities. Sometimes I have to wear a mask so that people don't recognise me. I have to be very brave every day to rescue those in need. I can never reveal my identity - never. So when I do good deeds, it's always Superman, never me!

Aiza Mannan (8)

Spring Cottage Primary School, Hull

The Town

One day in a town there lived a girl named
Ladybug, and there was also a boy named Agrion.
Ladybug and Agrion were good friends.
Agrion had an evil step dad. Ladybug and Agrion
both had superpowers, and they were superheroes
who knew what to do with evil people just like him.

Liyaa Hawar (8)
Spring Cottage Primary School, Hull

The Adventures Of Dot

Dear Diary,
Today I had an amazing day. I got up and barked at the mailman. Then I got my owner up. After that, I went for a nap. Then the most amazing thing happened. I woke up and I found myself in a cupcake land.

Isabella Coutts (7)
Spring Cottage Primary School, Hull

Space Girl's Diary

I was sitting in the pilot's seat blasting through space. Flying past planets in faraway galaxies. I was sitting next to my friend and he was an experienced astronaut. After many years of flying, I saw a blue and green planet. I looked it up and found out that it was called Earth. Using my third magnifying eye, I could see dots on the planet. What will these Earthlings be like? We crashed into this unknown place.

The thing with sticky-out bits said, "I'm Brian."

I said, "I'm Globlygloophead, an alien from Planet Zoombadoom. I'm returning home soon."

Ella Picken (9)
Swimbridge Primary School, Swimbridge

Zack Fire

Hi, I'm Zack, I was just a normal kid until last term I discovered I was not normal! I was half dragon, but more about that later. If you don't believe me, well then stop reading this book, but if you do then carry on. Now time to start the story.

"Zack, what is the answer to the question?" asked Mr Light, my history teacher.

"Pss... 1994," whispered my friend Alex.

"1994," I said to Mr Light.

Mr Light had fire-red eyes and a scraggly beard. He wore a polo shirt, jacket and black jeans. And that's when it happened...

Charile Parry (11)

Swimbridge Primary School, Swimbridge

Pesky Cat

Dear Diary,

Once there was a cat called Tango. Sometimes he's a very naughty cat and sometimes he's a very silly cat. When he's being a naughty cat he likes to chew my shoes. When he's being a silly cat he runs around the house really really fast.

He is a sneaky cat. He can sneak past me very quietly and I don't realise. Tango sleeps on my bed or he sleeps all over the house in funny places.

He is ginger and white. Tango is cute. He eats a lot of food. He's clumsy and a very pesky cat.

Alfie-Joe Blackmore (6)
Swimbridge Primary School, Swimbridge

The Curious Mermaid

It was a gorgeous summer's day and this morning I felt like feeling the warm sun on my skin. So I went up to the surface. On the way, I didn't notice the fishing nets and I got caught! I felt panicky and scared. Then I remembered what my parents told me, if there's a problem, see if you can solve it. I looked around and just then I saw my shell necklace. I took it off and used the sharp edge to cut the net and it worked! And I learned never to panic if there's an unexpected problem.

Penny Orr (7)
Swimbridge Primary School, Swimbridge

A Sparkly Shiny Crab Is Discovered

Dear Diary,

Yesterday I found a stripy, sparkly crab. I thought it was a new discovery because it was the only one there. I called it Tommy. When I found him, he crawled straight into my hands so I thought he liked me until my finger got bitten! That was only because I was all sandy. I took him home and put him in an old fish tank and bought new plants and toys for him. He only ate rainbow glitter cheese that he had in his claws but then I had to get more. Anyway, thank you, it's Amelia.

Amelia Darch (9)

Swimbridge Primary School, Swimbridge

Dear Diary

Dear Diary,

I woke up in my warm, dry bed. I fancied a nice morning swim and then breakfast. The place where I swim is a lake outside my house. When I got there, I put my head in the water and saw the weeds bobbing about. Then a noise announced my friend, bringing some breakfast. But my so-called friend decided to admire the land around my home but she didn't admire me or give me food! I got so sad, I pulled her shoelaces and she fell over. She screamed. Being a goose is so very hard.

Tom V H (10)

Swimbridge Primary School, Swimbridge

Magic School

Last Wednesday I went to my new school but when I got there I realised... it was magic! Suddenly I had a wand in my hand! First I went to a potions lesson, it was cool! But... when I went outside, it was cracking. I told everyone but no one believed me! I ran to the potions lab and I found a fixing potion. I ran outside and realised I could not reach it so I ran up 60,000,000 stairs and threw the potion at the magic school. Suddenly everyone started running out of the building very fast!

Anise Grant (7)
Swimbridge Primary School, Swimbridge

A Day In The Life Of Daisy

So today I had my boring breakfast (chicken and veg flavour). After, I did some sleeping. Later that morning (around 12:30) my pet took me on a walk to Coddon Hill. At the top, we stopped by the monument for a bit to have a rest then plodded on back to the car. Suddenly my doggo treats fell out of my pet's pocket so I gobbled them all up. When we got home I was sick. My sick was rather smelly. I was really tired because we walked like 2,000 miles (not really, it was like two).

Leila Pavord (11)

Swimbridge Primary School, Swimbridge

This Is Me

Dear Diary,

Once there was a guinea pig, a kitten and me. I was at school with my guinea pig and my kitten. Suddenly there was a lonely turtle called Swimming. Next to it was a lead and a golden trophy. I picked it up and gave it to the head teacher. She was surprised. She felt like she had happy tears. "Thank you!" she said. "Lunchtime!" she said happily.

At lunchtime she had lettuce. She shared it with my guinea pig. She had spare cat food.

Alex Ward (5)

Swimbridge Primary School, Swimbridge

YOUNG WRITERS INFORMATION

We hope you have enjoyed reading this book – and that you will continue to in the coming years.

If you're the parent or family member of an enthusiastic poet or story writer, do visit our website **www.youngwriters.co.uk/subscribe** and sign up to receive news, competitions, writing challenges and tips, activities and much, much more! There's lots to keep budding writers motivated!

If you would like to order further copies of this book, or any of our other titles, then please give us a call or order via your online account.

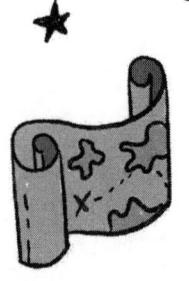

Young Writers
Remus House
Coltsfoot Drive
Peterborough
PE2 9BF
(01733) 890066
info@youngwriters.co.uk

Join in the conversation!
Tips, news, giveaways and much more!

 YoungWritersUK  YoungWritersCW  youngwriterscw

Scan to watch the
Incredible Diary Video